Accession no.
D0581906

More Sawn-Off Tales

Also by David Gaffney

SHORT STORIES

The Half-Life of Songs (Salt, 2010)

Aromabingo (Salt, 2007)

Sawn-Off Tales (Salt, 2006)

NOVEL

Never Never (Tindal Street, 2008)

DAVID GAFFNEY

More Sawn-Off Tales

SALT

CROMER

PUBLISHED BY SALT
12 Norwich Road, Cromer, Norfolk NR27 0AX United Kingdom

First published by Salt, 2013

Printed in Great Britain by Clays Ltd, St Ives plc

Typeset in Sabon 11/16

ISBN 978 1 907773 43 3 hardback

1 3 5 7 9 8 6 4 2

For Clare

Contents

Acknowledgements

SEVERAL OF THE stories in this collection were commissioned by Poole Literature Festival for the Poole Confessions project, and several appeared in *Ambit* magazine. In addition, Bleached Lichen Number Four, Everything's West Of Something, The Receipt and It Happens Inside appeared in *Stand* magazine. Something Happened Here, The Big Pub, The Three Rooms In Valerie's Head, It's All In Storage and Functional Market Area appeared in *Flash* magazine. Hidden Obvious Typical was a commission for *Station Stories 2011* and The Receipt appeared in Manchester Book Market's ebook for Comma Press in 2012. The Listed Bridge was a commission for *Quickies*, an anthology of smutty fiction, Effective Calming Measures appeared in *Stepaway* magazine, The Clever People Who Can't Do Anything Useful appeared in *Gutfire* magazine, Bonding was a commission for *Jawbreakers*, a collection to celebrate the first National Flash-Fiction Day, and New Audiences was commissioned by the Bugged project.

Thanks to my lovely daughters, Hannah and Sarah, for their never-ending support, and to my mother, Kathleen. Much appreciation goes to the following writers and friends for their support and encouragement: Peter Wild, Sian Cummins, Valerie O'Riordon, Sarah-Clare Conlon, Benjamin Judge, Nick Thompson, Nicholas Royle, Sally Dixon, and all at Bad Language and FlashTag. Thanks to Laura Simms-Luddington and Steve Simms-Luddington for their support of my musical project Les Malheureux, which features some of the stories in this collection. Finally, thanks to Sarah-Clare Conlon for her thorough and professional proofreading.

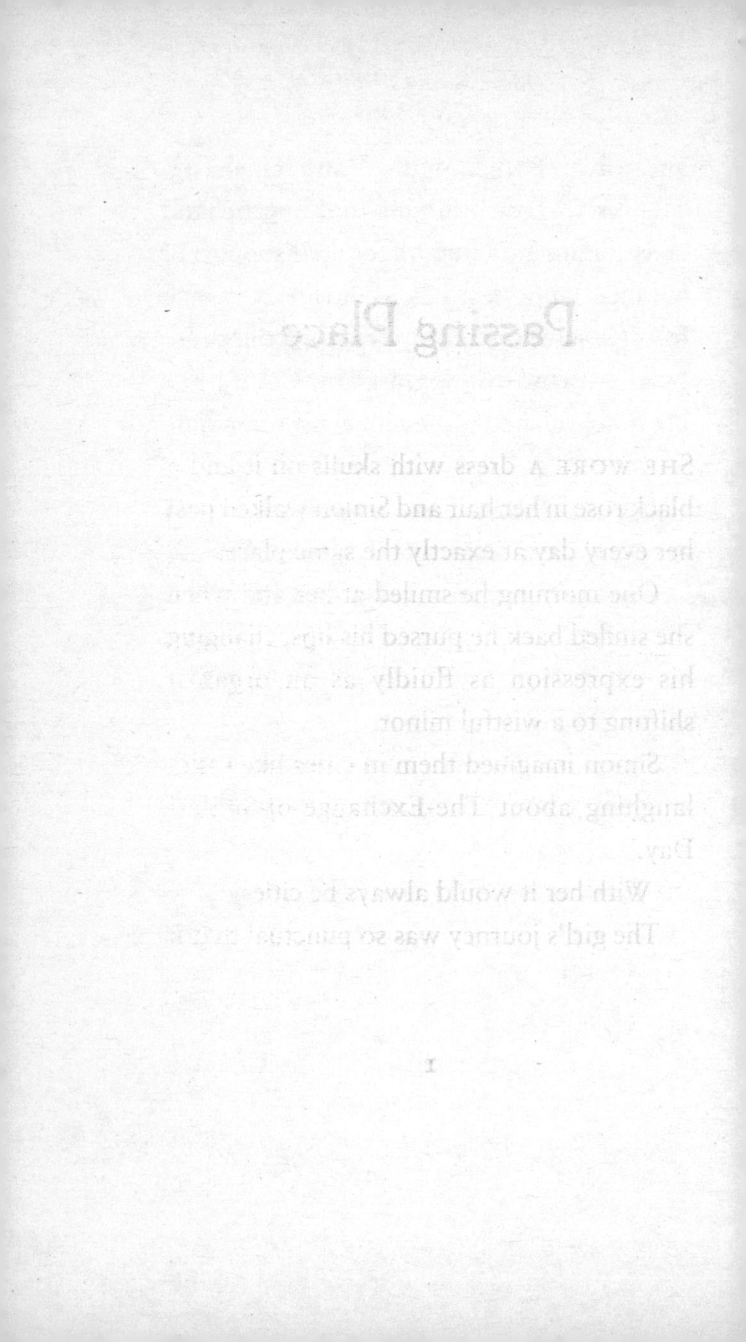

Passing Place

SHE WORE A dress with skulls on it and a black rose in her hair and Simon walked past her every day at exactly the same place.

One morning he smiled at her and when she smiled back he pursed his lips, changing his expression as fluidly as an organist shifting to a wistful minor.

Simon imagined them in cities like Oslo, laughing about The-Exchange-of-Smiles-Day.

With her it would always be cities.

The girl's journey was so punctual that it

could be calibrated to the second, and one day Simon stopped her.

'Look,' he said, and tore off his wristwatch and threw it into a bin.

She stared at him, and because she had no timepiece to discard, Simon unclipped the rose from her hair and tossed it into the road.

He hasn't seen her since and hasn't replaced his wristwatch, preferring to tell the time by peering into cars.

Nerves

IT WAS THE first time they'd spent an evening in together and Francesca was watching the darts while Ian pretended to read a book about the Korean famine.

Ian didn't know that Francesca liked watching darts.

She admired a player called Wolfy who was as calm as a boulder. When Wolfy checked out with a double sixteen, he would wag a stiff index finger at the audience and nod his head, unsmiling.

A tungsten dart weighs twenty-three grams.

The oche is the loneliest place in the world.

Darts is where romance and engineering intersect.

These were the facts Francesca liked about darts.

'Are you OK?' Ian called over. 'With us sitting and not speaking like this?'

'Yes,' she said. 'I'm fine.'

'I'm fine too,' he said.

Seventeen minutes passed and he called over again.

'It's good, isn't it? Being together but doing separate things?'

'Yes,' she said. 'It's all right.'

Hidden Obvious Typical

I PILED ALL the cards we'd ever exchanged on top of my bedclothes and every night slept underneath them.

It reminded me.

But after a while the cards seemed to be multiplying as if someone was adding to them as I dozed, so I took them to the railway station where I'd met her.

It wasn't long before they found the case, and the blast was like a stifled sob.

I looked down the tracks. There's a sense

of endless possibility about trains; you can change your life profoundly by stepping into a carriage. But nothing is random, nothing is unexpected. Everything about a train is predictable. Every train is on a track and every track connects to every other track, and every person on every train is connected to every other person on every other train and all things are certain.

I'm not sure you can control an explosion.

It Happens Inside

SHEILA WAS A radiologist and she liked to steal things from her neighbour's flat and X-ray them at work.

The first thing she took was his stuffed pheasant because she was interested in how the bird was held together.

She discovered that metal rods stood in for bones and there was something solid like a marble at the centre of its cranium. Next she X-rayed his nose-hair trimmers and his porcelain model of a VW van.

An invisible world lay within these objects, a secret universe. Once she had seen inside all of his things, she knew him better than anyone. That's when she decided to knock on his door and tell him all about it.

She had a folder with the X-rays in it and knew he would be fascinated by the images.

In his bedroom she would tell him everything about the contents of his pillows.

Oasis Leisure Lounge

As soon as the wives were out of earshot, Gareth leaned over to Howard and said in a conspiratorial tone, 'Hey, Howard, we have something in common.'

Howard laughed, awkwardly. He'd invited Gareth out because he'd been advised that if he became more socially engaged with his subordinates they would see him as a human being and not just a blob on an organogram.

'Oh, yes?'

'Yes.' Gareth leaned forward again and

said in a hissy high voice he thought no one could hear, 'We both have fat wives.'

He grinned. 'Eh? Eh? They are both very fat, and we are both slim. It's something we should talk about. A bond.'

Over Gareth's shoulder Howard spotted the wives returning from the toilets and he noticed Belinda smiling at a waiter. Her face was so beautiful and vibrant it broke his heart sometimes to know what people thought, what people said.

Bleached Lichen Number Four

LAURA PAINTED EVERYTHING in her house the same colour. Bleached Lichen Number Four. Walls, ceilings, woodwork, furniture. Even the wooden rings on the curtain poles.

She said it made the place look bigger.

Later, when our spark had gone and it was necessary to get a flat on my own, I had an idea.

If I smothered my stuff in Bleached Lichen, maybe a deep atomic magnetism would draw us back together.

Laura's walls would tingle, then throb, then tighten around her like a pulsing throat.

She would abruptly tug her head out of the *Guardian* Family section and sit bolt upright. Her slim frame would rise, open the door, and she would sniff the air.

Then, like a deer terrified of some unknowable static, she would drive recklessly and fearlessly to an address she didn't know and thump on the door.

And we could start at the beginning again.

The Clever People Who Can't Do Anything Useful

SOME PEOPLE ARE born with an innate flair for an art form not yet invented. Although immensely talented, they are unable to demonstrate their skills. These people can't even do a slot on Reggae Tuesday without telling a customer to 'fuck off, it's all dancehall 45s' when they ask for *Dreadlock Holiday*.

What can these people do?

They can press their faces into yours and

squeeze your arm with urgency. They can hold down portfolio careers.

Do they ever find each other?

Yes. And that is an improvement for a short period. But eventually they destroy their new friend because they detest what is locked within.

Where do they live?

They live among us, in places like Hebden Bridge.

Do they dance?

Not even at Latin-themed leaving dos.

What happens to them?

Eventually they die, usually early. That is what happens to these poor people and there is no cure.

Mo's Feet

At the time of the hearing, a barrister's assistant called Mo used to pick me up every day and take me to court.

Mo's shoes were sleek and elegant, like the spout of a Deco teapot or the wing of a vulture, and she used to remove them before driving because she could sense the speeds and the changes better in stockinged feet. She always handed them to me and asked me to toss them into the back.

Mo's feet were clever, too. She told me she was able to unwrap an Easter egg with her toes.

One day I might see, she said.

Mo made me forget about my predicament for a time.

If a female newsreader was on the radio, I imagined her rubbing the sole of a nylon-sheathed foot on the leg of the table while she spoke.

I pictured the newsreader doing this when she said my name.

The Zoo With Three Animals

MY MOTHER TOLD me about the zoo with three animals. It was called Preston Pleasure Gardens and there was a baboon, a monkey and an ostrich. I thought it was a shame that the baboon and monkey were the same type of animal as it made it appear that the zoo had only two animals.

But really it had three.

I used to walk around the zoo at Chester wishing I was at Preston Pleasure Gardens looking at the three animals. I would spend an hour with each, just staring at it, contemplating.

Now I have my own children and when I take them to the zoo I instruct them to look at three animals only; they can choose which.

'But a family ticket is forty-five pounds,' they say. 'How much is that per animal?'

This makes me think about unit costing and the disagreement with their mother over condoms.

Acceptable for Men to Like

SHE NOTICES THAT he reads *Sight & Sound*, and she likes that, because film is the only art form it's acceptable for men to like.

She hears him chat about jackets with frogmouth pockets.

She likes it that he doesn't smell of Shake n' Vac and knows he will keep his cheese in the fridge, because THAT'S NORMAL.

She thinks that he lives in a tunnel and eats rust.

When she follows him she makes her steps

in time with his. It helps her to experience the pavement the way he does. She has learned not to follow a man into his workplace.

Yesterday she rang him and stared at the phone with his name illuminated on it.

Semen oozed out of the speaker.

She imagined him leaning against scaffolding like a chained-up white rhino on *Relentless*.

She's tried dating sites but the men on there can't even spell Led Zeppelin.

Something Happened Here

Izzy said that she was willing to have sex with me only if it was in an empty property that we didn't own. This was just the way she was, terrified of permanence.

So we made an appointment and dressed appropriately and the twenty-something estate agent happily agreed to leave us alone to test the 'vibe'.

We did it three times — once in an unplumbed Jacuzzi, once on the kitchen units, and once on the living room floor.

Afterwards, we lay together imagining the psychic effect on the building's structure. They say that an orphanage has sadness in the walls; well, we had injected some love into the brickwork. This was a service we could provide professionally. Like the aroma of coffee, the echoes of recent sexual activity could be a powerful subliminal sales technique and I made a note to suggest it to a property consultant.

Reekers

MELTED HOOVES, BOILED beaks; Eileen worked at the gelatine factory and Sebastian grew erotically attached to her stink. So when she announced she was going to Bangor and a break was appropriate, he was appalled.

This was her father talking, this was Boylan's stretched-out kazoo voice.

He found Boylan in The Swan, but before Sebastian could speak, Boylan brought out a brown-stained square of paper, punished from years of folding, and held it up.

'Pick one,' Boylan said.

Different ballpoints had been used and

the first name was smeared, but Sebastian knew this was it.

The list of girls who smelled of their jobs.

Sebastian chose and Boylan said, 'Good boy', in a tone like a toy being strangled under water.

Outside The Swan, Sebastian skipped into the air. He just hoped the smell would linger after showering and thought about the toilet that the grave diggers used.

Functional Market Area

I HELPED IVAN load the eyes into his van.

'Why,' I asked him, 'is the order always the same? Surely there can't be a regular requirement for exactly the same number and type?'

'Everything ticks along,' Ivan grunted.

But he loved driving the eyes. He would tell everyone about his strange cargo, intoxicate women with stories of eyes for devil dolls and empty eye-socket fetishists, then have peculiar sex with them, involving our eyes.

He kept a glass eye himself, from a woman he was in love with, and he said it had a pleasant aroma like the underside of a wristwatch that hadn't been taken off for years.

I suspected there were no real customers for the eyes and that when Ivan finished with his women he tossed the eyes into some deep river and there they lay—teddybears' eyes, dolls' eyes, human eyes, staring at the fish.

More Men Will Come

I LEFT MY wife and moved into a converted barrel organ factory opposite a building with a giant orange illuminated question mark on its side.

This punctuation mark was the first thing I saw when I woke, and I hated it.

I decided to trap a pigeon and arrange for it to electrocute itself on the sign. I laid some pizza crusts inside a box, placed it near to where the pigeons played, and propped the lid open with a stick.

But the birds ignored it.

This was hopeless. Even if my plan

worked, men would repair it. And if I put these men in the ground, more men would come.

Then I looked up at the question mark and noticed that it was reversed. Its tone would be half-falling: not 'why' but 'if only'.

Suddenly, I hated the sign less and decided to celebrate it as a feature.

The Homes of Others

Ethel was a home worker, but her own flat was no place for industry with its mounds of bras and pizza boxes, so instead she worked in other people's houses.

She would wait until the occupants left, slide a credit card under the Yale, then creep onto the sofa with her laptop and tap away at the day's demands.

But today the numbers hypnotised her and she fell asleep. She woke up suddenly to find a man lying on the carpet holding her ankle tightly as if gripping a rail on a lurching train.

His eyelashes were ginger filaments, almost invisible, and he smelt of cannabis.

'I thought you were my step-sister,' he said.

'I just work here,' said Ethel.

He loosened his clasp.

'I didn't know I had another family. It's like finding out you have an extra limb. You don't know what it's for.'

Another chewed-up orphan with a perma-dusk past. They make the greatest boyfriends.

It's All in Storage

Don steered Martha onto the balcony where they leaned against the rail and looked out over acres of mothballed building sites, a blasted landscape of rusty foundation pins and hard core.

The knobs of Martha's spine felt like doll plastic through her blouse. She didn't stop his fondling. But when electronic music began to patter and bleep from the flat, it made her wince.

'Music for half-regenerated brownfield sites,' she said. 'I've got better.'

Her lips brushed his earlobe and she

sucked in air like a stifled cry of shock before beginning to sing.

The tune had an irregular time signature and no phrase repeated, it just wound round and round itself, over and over, always different and always the same, beautiful and endless.

When she stopped he felt her breath condense to cold moisture in his ear and he looked out over Ancoats and wondered if the builders would ever return.

Everything's West of Something

'HERE, CATCH,' I said, and time slowed down as the vase arced through the air.

You can discover everything about your girlfriend by tossing a breakable object towards her. Is she poised? Confident in her judgements? Does she seem willing to take responsibility for someone else's actions? Is she comfortable with spontaneity? What is her attitude to risk, debt, transgression, sin, guilt? How does she experience the passing of time? Does she appear to believe in an afterlife? An interventionist god? Ghosts, fate, predestination? Does she demonstrate a belief that character is learned? Is she concerned with the existential?

You learn most if the object belongs to someone else.

Watch the vase, watch the girl, and you will know all these things. And you will find out if she loves you.

We looked at the porcelain shards, then out through the rain-speckled window. The gate said *West Woods*.

She was the first girl I'd dated whose house had no number.

The Three Rooms In Valerie's Head

VALERIE'S MIND HAD three rooms: a front, a back and a cellar.

If there was something she didn't want to think about at a particular moment, she would move it into the back.

Then she could concentrate on playing the viola or explaining her job to her mother.

The problem was the cellar.

Sometimes she would bring three or four ex-boyfriends up from the cellar and arrange them into scenes—a trad-jazz band, or a dispute around a pool table—and she would move their jaws and make them speak in scratchy voices.

'Valerie was lovely, wasn't she.'

'Yes.'

'I wish I'd never left her.'

'We are all so stupid.'

Even though they smelled and had clouded weasel eyes and spongy biceps, it was good to imagine they were dead and position their bodies into these tableaux.

The drawback was having no space in the front room for anything else.

The Big Pub

It was one of those monsters with football on and fruit machines beeping and glossy burger offers.

Spandau Ballet played.

'The barber said you get a lot of fanny in here,' I said.

'Can I get you a drink?'

'Yes. Surprise me.'

He filled a glass from a pump.

'Last month I went to a unisex. She washed my hair with her fingers.'

The barman handed me a pint of pale yellow liquid.

'Like a head massage.'

'Three pounds,' the barman said.

'I used to visit pubs like this a lot, to grind knives. Who grinds your knives?'

He didn't know.

I took a sip. It was sweet. It didn't taste like the sort of thing I would drink. It tasted like something a junior solicitor would drink. I looked at my shoes.

Maybe I was a junior solicitor.

I downed it in one and set off for the coach.

The Joke About Todd Pokato

I ALWAYS MISPRONOUNCED Todd's surname as Po*kay*to hoping his receptionist would correct me. Then I could say, well, you say Pok*aar*to I say Po*kay*to.

But she always just said take a seat.

Years later my girlfriend chucked me and after a celebration drink for a promotion that should have been mine, I missed my stop, ended up in Doncaster, and spent eight hours in a kebab shop with Turkish TV and thick sweet coffee, thinking.

These problems were the fault of that unborn joke pulsing within me.

I rang every Pokato in the phonebook, but none bit. I tried online dating, but all Pokato people seemed cemented into banal coupledom.

Finally, I lied to Pokato's Tree Care about an unruly eucalyptus, called him round, and locked him in the garage.

Then I paced the floor, scowling. I'd become used to the rotting quip inside. Was I ready to release it?

Lifting and Handling the Truth

George worked alone, making library music for corporate DVDs, and he hated his job and his solitary existence. Lunchtimes watching the price of one pint tapped into the till while the barmaid, with routine intimacy, tickled the barman's back with spider fingers; customers who want everything to sound like Boards of Canada.

One day he was copying a file and watching the fill-line creep up when he thought about the time he and Janet stayed on Skerryvore while George installed the seal microphones.

The island was accessible only by rowing boat, but despite the danger, neither of them learned to swim.

Who would want the responsibility of saving the other's life?

George missed the *frisson* of risk.

He removed the power plug from his keyboard and jammed the bare wires into the socket.

Maybe later he would fly a kite near a pylon, or skate on a frozen quarry.

He would see.

The Building With the Hole

I MOVED INTO a building with a hole in the middle. The hole was a yawning chasm where the centre flats had their balconies: gloomy yards in the sky that got hardly any sun apart from a tickle in the afternoon and a few dying rays last thing.

Hester lived in one and she said sunshine was like a friend: at its best on first meetings and farewells.

I was lucky and lived on a corner. But still I hated this gaping hollow. It was like perpetual hunger, a hum, an emptiness never to be filled.

One evening Hester called down from the shadows of the hole. Tonight was barbequed heart and homebrew and did I want to join her?

I said yes.

Maybe I could plot with Hester and find a way to fill in the hole. This would help us develop skills for when the economy picked up again.

The Proper Care of Surfaces

Jessica adored her Melody Boy radio, but I couldn't see its attraction. It was the sort of drab appliance a team of decorators would listen to while refreshing the interior of a Spud-U-Like in Warrington.

It stood next to the hob and to prevent it from splatters she covered it with a tea towel when we cooked.

'Just drape it with a tea towel. What's so difficult?'

But whenever Jessica raced into the kitchen

unannounced, there I was, showering the naked receiver in a storm of hot flying oil.

She used tea towels to protect other things.

Her Debenhams linen placemats were to keep her B&Q dining table nice, but she didn't want the placemats grubbed up so would lay tea towels over them too.

'We are eating off towels,' I said.

In the quilted orange parka and wellingtons she was wearing over nothing else, she squinted at me like Forest Whittaker looking at a Magic Eye picture.

The Receipt

WE MADE A creature out of the things we liked, but the creature died. I put the creature on the bed and examined it. It was clear we hadn't done a good job. The joints between some of the elements were crude, and several of the pieces didn't fit together properly at all, like someone had got bored with a jigsaw of the sky and jammed pieces in haphazardly so no clouds were complete and there were marooned fragments of fluff in wide expanses of blue.

No wonder the poor thing had perished. But all was not lost. We could dismantle it and start again. That's what everyone else did. They rebuilt their creatures over and over until they were shiny and scampered about the house whooping and clawing at the furniture.

But when I suggested this all she did was kiss me, and the kiss was like a receipt.

The Smell Comedian

BOYLAN WAS A smell-comedian at the deaf and blind club and because his act was bawdy, he collected his funniest smells from the local brothel. The Madame would infuse his cloths with dense, curdled aromas which, when delivered with precision timing by his smell amplification system, elicited huge laughs.

But modern audiences wanted darker material. They yearned for the whiffs of unmet desire, of false hope, of nothingness. Positioned correctly these modern smells were hilarious and disturbingly true.

The salesman was thin and wore a safari suit. He snicked open the catches of a silver briefcase to reveal coloured cloths sealed tightly in plastic wallets.

Later, Boylan tossed the coloured cloths onto his fire and his nostrils prickled with the carbonised atoms of nothingness. The girl would be home soon and she didn't like Boylan's smells.

Young people don't need comedians, she would say. Everything is funny when you're young.

Get the Ball and Give It to Bobby Moore

I WAS A book recovery officer for the council. The tomes I liberated were stuffed with colour plates of extinct beasts and mysterious cartography and I liked to press my cheek against the leather and breathe in their damp earthiness.

My job was simple. Locate books, return books. Like Nobby Stiles' job for United: get the ball and give it to Bobby Moore. That's what I said to myself when some hysterical customer wailed about prosecution or monstrous fines.

Morality wasn't my job. If every worker pondered the intergalactic purpose, nothing would ever get done.

One night I was looking at a watercolour of a lemon and turquoise Lady's Slipper orchid and I imagined it cloaked forever in darkness, viewed only through the pin-eyes of mites. Then suddenly I was next to it, flattened and sucked dry like extinct grass, and I couldn't imagine what Nobby would say about that.

The Gypsy in Me

'HE WILL EXPLODE into song at the water cooler and dance a polka in meetings.'

Vanessa loved the idea of The Gypsy In Me and her eyes glittered as she spoke.

'Girls will love him because they will sense,' she took a big breath, 'the gypsy in him!'

'No,' I said.

'It's a story about a man with a small gypsy living inside him.'

'Like an elf?' The spaces between her words grew longer as if she were talking to me on a satellite connection. 'An elf only he can see? That pops out from behind his ear and tells him to do gypsy things?'

'No,' I said.

On the way home I filled in the gaps. It would be a realistic gypsy who was training to become an optician. A Ken Loach-type project. The gypsy would sleep in the folds of the man's coat. That's what the 'in' part means.

New Audiences

ALFIE RAN THE Sadler's Wells café concession when I was in *Giselle with Tractors*.

'If it wasn't for these tractor drivers my business would be dead,' he said. 'You fuckers in tights buy nothing but Mint Aeros and fags.'

I liked the tractor drivers. They had fat dirty fingers, sexy bald heads, and good tyres on their cars.

And Alfie was right, they ate like rats. Black pudding, fried bread, liver in gravy, Arctic roll, the lot. Us dancers watched them ladling down gristle while we lapped at unfeasibly tiny yogurts, and it was like looking at a filthy film.

But dancing with heavy machinery was a blip and the tractors had to leave, so to remind Alfie of the good times I gave him a Ladybird book about farming.

'We both need strong men in our lives,' he said and placed the book on the counter for everyone to see.

The Power of Millions

On our second date we broke into the derelict pump house at the old mine and Brett threw himself on all fours and touched the ground with his tongue.

'That's Ministry of Defence Tarmac,' he declared, standing up and wiping the grit from his mouth.

His beautiful curls glowed in the moonlight and I thought, what an idiot.

In the control room Brett's torch revealed buckled gauges, rusted levers, and minuscule numbers scribbled on the walls.

He switched off the light then kissed and

fumbled at me. The air seemed to thicken so I pushed him away.

'That doesn't make sense, Brett. The Tarmac being Ministry of Defence. This was a coal mine.'

He sparked a Lucky and I felt smoke on my face.

'Yes,' he said, 'it's sinister,' then flipped on the torch again.

Its beam had the power of two million candles and I pictured them filling a cathedral.

Boy You Turn Me

I GOT WITH Vince when Natural World opened and we split up when it closed.

Natural World was supposed to get us away from plastic and chemicals. But the world isn't natural. Orchids are made of chemicals, so are foot spas, torture devices, pork scratchings, guns and gold.

The rocks we took, the shells we took, the crystals, the wood, the sand we took. The loot. Maybe the natural world ran out, maybe we collected everything natural and there was nothing left, the entire natural world, scooped up, sealed into plastic bags, labelled, and flogged off. Every sparkly gem, every sea-smoothed chunk of driftwood.

I don't remember much now, just blurs of colour like lights caught in long exposures.

He smoked strong cigarettes and liked old films.

We went for walks.

We would go for miles.

Drinking alcohol and caffeine.

And cackling at things that weren't funny.

And holding on tight.

It Doesn't Really Matter If Things Die Out

EVERYTHING IN THE future was as I expected.

No one had a job because everybody made their own things with 3-D printers. Tweets could be turned into wearable jewellery and emotional data into liquid. The high street had died, as had saucers and certain blue-coloured insects. But none were missed.

A sought-after delicacy was feral lamb. Farmers could make everything they needed with their 3-D printers so their neglected sheep skulked about the town with the urban otters, eating out of bins.

Hunted on quad bikes with crossbows, and butchered with rusty saws in empty high-rises, feral lamb was an exquisite meat, with multi-layered notes of pepperoni and chip fat and the aroma of wet soil after a hurricane.

You could plug yourself into a machine that made you think you were eating it, but it wasn't the same.

Taped Over

You had taped over it. Hadn't thought, hadn't asked.

I remember doing the same thing.

Before the days of Gary Glitter, I used my leatherette-sheathed cassette recorder mainly to record myself humming.

But one day I Sellotaped over the protection tabs of my mother's C30 and slipped it in.

The music had been important to her—a dozen Les Pauls dancing around a choir of Mary Fords—and this loss, on top of the fact that Dad had just ditched her for The Blinker, made her incandescent.

Now one of my own treasures was blotted out.

I did my sulky mouse and rammed the tape into the machine.

Nothing but run-off. Scratchy antique jingles for ancient products, pre-publicity for forgotten shows.

I thought about Les Paul and Mary Ford, quipping over pancakes before trotting hand in hand to their studio.

I cover you with a new one, but you still show through.

Thrill Me Slowly

He hopped on the 48 at The Dread and the first thing you noticed was the glove: white and dotted with sequins, it was an unusual garment for Esh, a gnarly ex-mining town where I'd once photographed a couple getting married in sportswear and slippers.

His doomy, freckled face made him look as if he would predict terrible things if you met him in the smoking area of an indoor car-boot sale, and he appeared to relish the incongruity of his twinkling glove.

I filmed him, of course, but by the time I found out he was fifteen and had an artificial hand, it was too late. I'd made him dance to the slow version of *Thriller* and posted the clip to the world.

That night I watched it over and over. *Thriller* sung slowly seems to boil with madness, spite and loss. The word 'midnight' means so much more.

The Listed Bridge

MY PENIS GREW so huge I became housebound, and every time I got stuck in an awkward position my mother was quick to call the firemen.

During their manoeuvres I sometimes became erect and the firemen would climb up on it and sit in a row swinging their legs. One wore tiny square spectacles and chatted to my mother about the terrible congestion in Kendal.

'It's because the listed bridge is too weak for two-way traffic,' he said, and my mother agreed.

Later we called the firemen again. I was able to climax only with the aid of a physical theatre company, and although I'd warned the girls, one was new, and now she was hanging on the wall like an aphid in cuckoo spit.

My mother blamed the listed bridge for making the men late.

But I saw something in the girl's eyes, something like a prayer.

The Good Machines

PHOEBE COULDN'T SLEEP because the cooling fan in her laptop had broken.

Its regular whooshing was like music, giving the silences between each burst a shape, a weight, and a meaning.

But the IT man said Phoebe's laptop didn't need a fan. The manufacturer discovered the public bought certain laptops because they had fans, and even though the engineers swore it was unnecessary, the management insisted they install one.

'Apparently,' he laughed, 'we are soothed by pointless trimmings.'

Phoebe smashed her phone against the wall.

A laptop that didn't whirr would be like some sullen lodger who never interacts unless directly addressed.

She fetched her hairdryer and cuddled it between her thighs. It felt pleasantly hard and cold and, because it had the capability to emit a similar noise, it helped.

Phoebe needed to hear the sounds of helpful machines and if she couldn't, she would just have to imagine.

Happy Birthday, Hee Hee

As Jim was leaving, Martha called out to him, 'Have a good birthday,' and after he'd gone, I said, 'I didn't know it was Jim's birthday.'

'It's not,' she said.

I'd been brought in as a *plodder/mapper* for personality balance, but I just couldn't seem to gel. I didn't understand that *come and chomp down on our networks* meant join them for a drink, or why they said *afternoons are the new evenings*, or *wah-wah factor*, or *Gooorrn fishun*.

Each time our digital pet Coochy died because we'd forgotten to stroke it, a bloke pulled out a trumpet and played Telstar, and when the new Coochy was installed, they made a remote control helicopter dance to an Italian porn movie soundtrack.

'It's not Jim's birthday,' Martha explained. 'It's just something we say around here.'

'So what do you say,' I asked, 'when it really is someone's birthday?'

'We don't say anything.'

The Scientific Explanation for Faraway Eyes

DANIEL WAS A rationalist and knew there was no such thing as faraway eyes. But in the case of Alison, her faraway eyes had been his obsession.

His new girlfriend, Paula, a maid at the hotel, had lovely eyes, but they could never be called faraway.

Late at night, when the rest of the hotel staff were drinking and getting up to mischief in the scullery, he would zoom in on a photograph of Alison's eyes. But there was no clue as to what made them faraway.

Eyes could be removed from their sockets with a melon-baller. Daniel had seen it in a war film. He could keep them on ice like in transplant documentaries, drape a hotel room in plastic sheets, then hire a surgeon to implant them into Paula.

But in someone else's head would they still look faraway? It was a risk he would have to take.

Can You Feel the Waves?

Bored with empty houses, Izzy became desperate to have sex while someone else was in the room. But she didn't want this third person to see her farm-girl calves, so the blind piano tuner, with his swimmy spectacles as thick as if they'd been cut from the shark tank at the aquarium, was perfect.

As he began to strum the keys, Izzy removed her clothes and crept towards me like a foal tiptoeing through snow. Then she crouched down and I entered her from behind and we moved, then stopped, moved then stopped. At times we were still as a monument.

Until there was an enormous bang and a string flew up, twitching like an electric cable.

I listened to the silence and I guessed the piano tuner did too. But was it the same for him?

The creaking of timber, the moan of wind through glass.

I heard everything.

Let's See What Rachel's Been Up To

RACHEL LOVED RICHARD Heaven and posted everything about him on Facebook.

Heaven knew the smell of spermicide like a tabby knows lion shit. Heaven whacked his dyspraxic son with a plastic bottle. Heaven once shagged a sweet wrapper.

Rachel was obsessed with Heaven and I became obsessed with her obsession.

Then one day they bickered about revival-ska, Heaven typed the word 'sigh', and the next night, in an urban park she'd never heard of, he told her it was over.

There was a Heaven-shaped gap on her sofa, and a photograph of a snowman sporting his trilby and a roll-up cigarette appeared titled 'When Heaven's Not Here'.

The evenings were long without Rachel's bulletins, so I persuaded my boyfriend Jason to message her about revival-ska and they agreed to meet.

Last night she uploaded a picture Jason had drawn of her, which he'd covered in glitter.

She called it sparkleicious.

Nothing Can Hurt Me Now

THE MESSAGE WAS to Hilary's mother from Roof-Voice.

Honeythighs.

For revenge, Hilary decided to sleep with all of her mother's ex-boyfriends, starting with first love Gavin, now a vet in Stoke-On-Trent.

She wondered if riding naked could have an adverse affect on her horse's hide. The fluids?

Gavin's face took on a cloudy look and she watched the lust sluicing through him.

Afterwards they drank port and listened to Bach.

'Pay attention to the complexity,' he said, 'not the surface.'

He had dancing eyes and long fingers.

She located Jez, a regeneration officer her mother lived with for six years, at the science-fiction book club and they whispered about robot love.

There was a lot of stuff, like he'd been storing it for decades, and it smelt like old wallpaper.

She pictured them in his 'n' hers Fruit of the Loom sweatshirts and decided to stay.

This would hurt her mother more.

Nineteen-Eighties Cavalier

I NEEDED SOMETHING easy to nick, and there it was, come-to-me-baby, a white 1980s Cavalier.

As usual, the door flipped open like butter and I was about to jump in when I spotted a scribbled Post-It pushed under the wiper blade.

Why is your car parked here, outside that bitch's place?

I chucked the note into the gutter and

drove away, spending the rest of the night on deliveries.

Around four in the morning I flipped off the headlamps, swung down behind the allotments, and rested it against a grass verge. Then I noticed a scrap of yellow left under the wiper: just the name Nicola and, oddly, a kiss.

I rang Cissy.

'What the fuck?' she said. 'It's four in the morning.'

'I just wanted to say I'll see you on Saturday.'

'I know you will,' she said, and I heard her yawn then put down the phone.

The Man Who Was Always There But Never Said Anything

A FEW STEPS behind us in the park, next to us in the supermarket queue, a row in front at the cinema; he was a constant. He had a grizzled beard and a coat with a wolf on it and stared at us blankly as if we were on television.

Years passed and I grew accustomed to his presence.

He became our anchor. On the few

occasions he was absent, I felt shaky and nauseous.

One evening I went to see a Gondry film—alone, because my husband dismisses Gondry as senti-surrealist.

As usual the man was there, and at the end of the evening I spoke to him.

I asked if I could live with him and be with him all the time. He wouldn't need to speak, just follow me around.

We both knew by then that there was no room for my husband in our world.

Blood in Flight

MARIA'S HUSBAND, CARL, was a blood spatter analyst for the police.

If she spilled something, Carl always knew exactly what had happened; how she'd lost balance, the force of the fall, the amount of liquid involved. He could even tell whether Marie herself had spilt it or whether someone else had been round.

And because Maria worked as a prostitute, men often came on her face, and if she hadn't made a perfect job of cleaning it off, Carl would examine her under the hall light and tell her how far away the man was when he shot, the length of his cock, and even how old he was, all from the force of the ejaculation.

Is nothing private any more? Maria thought.

That's when she began to fake the spatters, and that's when Carl lost his confidence, and that's when he left the lab and set up running dispatch.

Lag Phase

I WAS WAITING for the waiter to deliver my Filet-o-Fish when a woman wearing a leather dress held together at the sides by laces appeared carrying my meal.

'Here you go, honey,' she said, 'I was on my way out and it saved the lad a walk.'

The woman was made of round edges and her skin was the colour of polished rice.

She contemplated me as if I were in a shop window and I looked at my fish sandwich, its baby-soft bun and yellow batter reminiscent of the trim on a Roberts radio, and couldn't eat. I felt alone and unmoored.

'I bought this for a *Rocky Horror* party,' she said, indicating her unusual garment, which creaked as she swayed and smelled of farms. 'But it's perfect for this weather.'

Then she handed me an ice-cream sundae.

'Have this,' she said. 'It was part of a deal.'

Buy Yourself a Cheap Tray

THERE WAS NO way eleven guests would fit round Ron's bijou dinner table, a melamine-coated contraption that folded out from the wall and was held up by a pole slotted into a recess in the floor.

What could he do instead?

The hole in his laminate waited for its pole, nagging at him like a hollow tooth. Then he came up with his masterstroke. Trays. Trays would be funny; trays would be ironic.

Everyone would explode.

Later that evening Ron solemnly handed out his jaunty plastic platters. One was adorned with a gyrating Cliff Richard, one a weightlifter in puce shorts, one a cute kitten in a washbasin.

'The *tray* we were,' said Sam.

'It's a *trayful* chilly in *heyare,'* said Emily.

'Gabba Gabba *Tray*,' said Ron.

Without the trays, the dinner party would have been grown-up; a word young people use to describe people who aren't having any fun.

Skewness

PRECISE CALIBRATION WAS important to our relationship and we were continually striving to quantify the length of time we'd been a couple.

Beatrice suggested we count it from our first meeting; but we didn't even brush fingertips. Or our second encounter when, although we had an intense conversation about Parisian cinemas, our dry, awkward kissing with spectacles clinking together didn't begin until seven minutes before my train.

I favoured the occasion nine weeks later

when she cried, 'Oh Fraser!' Like hearing my name spoken aloud for the first time.

But really I wanted to mark the moment we fell in love—for me, during a Godard film when a pang of delirious joy nearly hurled me out of my seat.

She won't agree that date, but it doesn't matter. I keep a ball of tissue under my armpit and drop shreds of it into her food to keep her loyal.

For The Lady

'SO,' SAID GRAEME, 'let's unpack this thing. Lay out the cogs and see how it works. We are enjoying a romantic meal. But what is romance? What is a meal? Think about the candle.'

He grabbed the crimson taper from the centre of the table and held it aloft like a baton.

'Animal blubber with string for a wick. A rudimentary method of lighting the gloom. Because it flickers? Because it masks imperfections?'

He lobbed the still-lit candle out of the window into the street.

'That object contains no love. A true romantic artefact is a magical talisman imbued with meaning extraneous to itself and its function. Emotional significance is accrued to it from a couple's joint experience of a tangible thing. If a couple fall in love while working at a slaughterhouse, the screams of terrified beasts will be romantic for them.'

'This is nice,' Henrietta said.

Other People's Worlds

I SEE THEM everywhere. They are of a type and share the same features.

Now that I know the damage they do, it is my duty to warn others.

I spoke to the boyfriend of one earlier while he was waiting outside a station ticket office.

I pointed at her and explained the characteristics and how they are manifested.

I told him what had happened with mine; what she had done.

The man stared at me for a long time and said nothing.

But the information went inside and stayed like radiation.

Later, I scoured the town for more.

Here was another, on a bench in front of the university fruit stall.

Her boyfriend was gripping her hand and they looked like they'd been arguing.

I followed them and, as soon as she was out of the way, I pounced.

I couldn't allow the misery I'd suffered to creep into other people's worlds.

Inches From What You Want

FERGUS WAS ON a trade union trip to Eastern Europe and it was sweltering hot, so after a dull lecture about the hard left's infiltration of mainstream parties, the men drank a large amount of cheap lager, then tore off their clothes and dived into the river where a natural dam and a rock bed had formed a deep, clear pool.

Fergus wasn't a strong swimmer and tended to float on his front, and it was then that he saw the eyes, thousands of them, staring up at him.

There were human eyes, fish eyes, reptile eyes and bird eyes, beady eyes for toy bears and giant eyes for dinosaurs, and all of these eyes seemed to be laughing at him.

It seemed unreal, like a photograph no one took, a memory no one has.

He got out of the water and dried himself roughly before heading back to the college.

Uncle Leonard

HIS SKILLED CURATION of Mossorama, a touring exhibition of moss from Darwin's collection, made Leonard famous. He was so obsessed with Mossorama he would pose as a visitor and ask invigilators how it was doing. They would laugh and say, well, to be honest we had high hopes, but it seems nobody is excited by moss any more.

Leonard is 60 now. Fat, diabetic, and addicted to flu-strength Paracetemol, he has no job, owns no property and is well out of the moss world. Categorising moss, he says, is a young man's game.

Why doesn't he have a woman? He is funny, has teeth, hair and a motorbike, and is an expert on 1930s science fiction. And moss. But who ever met a girl in the sci-fi section of a bookshop or at a moss exhibition?

Sometimes you have to accept that no one will ever love you.

The Bad Psychiatrists

They were bad men. We should have known from their names, Rick and Andy; like bass guitarists in a blues band.

But nobody noticed.

The two psychiatrists observed that bi-polar sufferers in manic phases went on spending sprees, buying expensive equipment they didn't need; in one instance a classic Bang & Olufsen Beomaster, with slider controls.

So the bad doctors arranged arts activities for these patients, and while the depressives were busy, broke into their houses.

I found a restaurant bill after one such sortie and they even had dessert.

Rick had the posset and Andy had the jelly.

The posset was rhubarb and ginger; the jelly, raspberry and rosé wine and, grinning like devils, the two psychiatrists would have licked the gloop off spoons as dainty as doll's cutlery.

Me, I tilt into an underworld and hide the receipts.

Even bad men have to eat.

But no one needs pudding.

This Is Your Brain On Drugs

'WOULD ANYONE MIND?' Masie aimed the remote at the stereo imploringly. 'It's an audio recording of a facelift.'

'Another sugar-doody for Master Boris,' said Boris.

But Masie half closed one eye and gave him her crooked smile, so he let her press the switch.

Scraping, folding, fluids tick-ticking, tissue squelching.

It was Christmas and Boris's parents

were round and they hated sonic sculpture as much as they hated holidays.

To battle through, Boris had really put a load on, and now the furniture was melting and a thousand claustrophobic hours stretched out like a traffic jam.

Later, Masie snoozed. Her usual creamy shoulders, her usual swan neck.

Boris took out his mobile, found her number, and hit delete.

Her sleeping face didn't alter.

It ought to hurt, your name spinning into oblivion, but no one feels anything any more. Even out here, even in the countryside, they were no closer.

Doll Parts

MICHELLE GOT A Sindy Casino for Christmas and I desired that set of gaudy plastic objects more than anything in the world.

I had a fat Asda mutant with clothes made from crisp bags.

Mother said I was shallow. Did I want pneumatic breasts, skeletal limbs, and an ant-sized waist? To end up with a mobile phone salesman on commission only who beat me with a bag of oranges every night?

I didn't.

But I did want Sindy Casino.

Michelle kept her dolls in sweet jars and that night in the fold-out I dreamed about blondes in glass dungeons lined up at the back of a betting shop. In one cell Sindy was gripping a roulette wheel between her legs and Paul was turning it with his tongue.

The display was managed by a man on commission only and he turned to me and smirked.

He had Nando breath and this made it better.

The Woman With the Four Planks of Wood

I WATCHED HER from the train. She wore a black and white diamond-patterned coat and was arranging four planks of wood into a neat stack on the floor. Suddenly she hoisted the planks up on to her shoulder as deftly as a majorette swinging a baton and marched off and, even though I was miles from my stop, I leapt off the train and followed her.

In a dusty upstairs room in The Blue Boar, I watched her place the four planks of wood on a low stage under a spotlight. Then she disappeared round the back.

I sat and looked at the four planks of wood. An hour went by and nothing happened, so I grabbed the planks of wood and ran for it.

Later I took the planks out to the garage, lashed them together with rope, and attached a note saying Do Not Burn.

Loss Function

Every time Hugh told a girl he worked in trauma analysis, she said the same thing.

So before his next date he made some observations.

He divided his ticks into intervals and discovered there was a laugh every 3.2 minutes.

But should the laughter be sustained and in unison? And should certain laughs be given different weightings? Like Brian's half-grunt-half-snort at the mention of ambulance arrival times. And what about Henry's wry smiles, or Aaron's raised eyebrows, or when

Horace said, in a bitter dolorous tone, 'Have you had a postcard from the dog?', and Maurice said *very satirical,* because Belter had crept into a van on its way to Dorset.

Nevertheless, Hugh was prepared for the next girl and as soon the words were said, he uncrumpled his spreadsheet.

But she was unimpressed.

Perhaps he needed clearer criteria. More probably he just hadn't thought about people who laugh inside.

The Bear's Head

SOME INSCRUTABLE FORCE within Fergus drove him to order a bear's head, but he was disappointed.

It didn't look fierce. The bear was snarling, but a strange curl on its lips gave it a sardonic air, like it was snarling in inverted commas.

There was a knowing, complex dimension to the beast's personality and this was not the effect Fergus desired.

So he drove it to The Feathers where it might sit well alongside the mongoose fighting a cobra.

'It looks left-wing,' the landlord said. 'A trendy bear that belongs in a wholefood café, not a pub.'

Fergus imagined the hunter preying on the fringes of bear society, on bears who might not have full community support.

He took the bear home and stowed it under the stairs.

He might never look at it again, but he would always know it was there, alone and dead, staring into the blackness.

Like a Town

THERE IS A place called Hope and people live there. Hope is a town where you can rot away from the inside and no one notices. Where the sky is the colour of aged Tupperware and tram doors close with a growling sound.

I don't live there now.

Towns release spores that become mini versions of themselves, so as well as Hope there is Great Hope, Hope Chapel, Hope Moor and Hope-on-the-Hill, and I live in one of them.

But Amanda stayed on.

She wondered why no one had thought of preserving enormous beasts like giraffes in resin and displaying them in Hope. Art should be used, she said, to thin the hedges between the fields.

She claimed the quality of false hope was now so improved that it was almost indistinguishable from real hope.

The Mousemats Say Innovate Or Die

THE GREASE MARK was on my thigh, a dark oval that popped out against the beige of my trousers, so I had to cover it.

Perhaps a badge. That's what the lads in big plastic spectacles and reindeer jumpers would do.

So I pinned *Knowsley, Home of QVC* to my leg and stood in front of the mirror, doing la-la-la.

It was unconvincing.

But then I had a brainwave.

I grabbed olive oil and a Q-tip, lay the trousers on the floor and dabbed them carefully with grease all over, making each stain exactly the same size and shape.

They were part of a suit so I did the jacket as well, and at FabLab everyone commented on my unusual fabric.

Even Emily Booth liked it, and she was working on a love bite machine for the hen party market that imprinted dirty words on your skin in big sucked-out bruises.

Normal Hours

OFTEN WE WERE seen in huddles discussing absurdist theatre. Sometimes, during an argument about cheese triangles, one of us might bite another man's nose clean off. If visitors were lucky they'd catch us on a dusky evening dancing together jerkily, and cameras would whirr like insect machines.

If a car stopped moving we would climb on top and leer in, showing stumpy teeth.

Snapped-off windscreen wipers became weapons to kill each other with when crazed from fear and loneliness.

But it was all right.

Our bodies were removed discretely, without recourse to law. Violent death was natural; the way trees crash down in forests.

Fires were lit in winter and postcards in the gift shop showed us in silhouette against the flames. The most popular was two men hugging in the rain while another absent-mindedly held an umbrella over them.

We each owned a copy and displayed it in our sheds.

Private View

COOL AIR BRUSHED my buttocks as the nurse opened the flap at the back of my gown and I heard the slip-slap of lubricant on the camera.

Then suddenly my anus became a gulping, gelatinous mouth and the tube wormed up inside me like a long, thin girl swimming up a pipe.

Into the grimy marshmallow it went and suddenly an awful emptiness loomed up and I gasped.

My art work had disappeared. The artist

had promised it would never deteriorate, always be there.

The gurney seemed to pitch and yaw under me.

'I'm sorry,' the nurse said in a voice that sounded refrigerated.

Back at the gallery I felt the warm gel drizzling out of me. I heard scoops of laughter from secret pockets of the building where I had no idea what went on. I could smell Worcester sauce crisps from the bin.

I was a normal man again.

Dip Finish

THE MAN FROM the government wore green seersucker shorts and he asked me to tell him all about my Olympics.

I explained that the Games would be held behind the boarded-up houses and would be for disadvantaged people. This information, however, seemed to land heavily on him, and he sighed deeply and shook his head.

I got the impression that the government didn't want the lower classes to become superfast sprinters or gain the ability to leap high fences and throw heavy objects, and

I'm sure he mumbled something about civil unrest.

I asked him if he would prefer it if we concentrated on sports like snooker, motocross or coarse fishing, and he seemed delighted by this. He promised us sweatshirts with Sony written on them.

'Elite sportsmen,' he said, 'require a psychic wound. That's what propels them. I suggest you help people from the council estate develop that first.'

DJ Stinger and the Ghost Alpcaca

THE FRENETIC GUT-FILTH roar from DJ Stinger next door was seriously disturbing my alpacas, so I went over.

'Just a little Detroit techno,' DJ Stinger drawled.

'Peters and Lee are the great-grandchildren of a pair brought over from Peru in the seventies. It's quiet there,' I said.

'Those alpacas would have heard proper bass in the seventies,' he said, and twirled a knob.

From a speaker the size of a hatchback, a bass pulse throbbed and I watched through the window as Lee quivered, then dropped.

Outside, I lay on the ground and pressed my cheek against the cold base of her hoof.

She went to a trustworthy renderer—I didn't want a repeat of the nipple-necklace—and I buried her head in DJ Stinger's garden.

He came round because he couldn't relax. There was something at the back of his neck—moist, panting, silky—but when he turned, nothing.

Effective Calming Measures

THE MINI-ROUNDABOUT AT Seldown Bridge holds three cars and has eight lanes of traffic channelled onto it. I looked at it for a long time. I saw the giant tin opener on the quay and thought about how much I miss the Hants and Dorset bus garage.

I could sleep the sleep of a thousand animals.

The man in purple velour staggered by playing *Danny Boy* on a mouth organ and I asked him if he ever dressed up as a butterfly catcher, but he just told me to stop whistling, even though I wasn't.

It was now necessary to make some adjustments to my life.

I went home and set fire to the neighbours' shed, laughing as it burned and warming my hands on the flames. They watched from the window, pressing numbers into a little phone.

All I am waiting for is some intelligence to come out of the mouths of council staff.

How to Get Around in the Sky

DOMINIC LEANED FORWARD across the table. 'The more passengers on an aircraft who are afraid of flying, the more likely it is to crash.'

Thump.

'Fact.'

Forty had slammed up hard against Dominic and he fought it by becoming a pilot, flying oil barons in and out of Equatorial New Guinea where deposits had been discovered.

'Brains are just clumps of electric pulses,' I said. 'So I guess it's possible that dozens of passengers experiencing intense fear could affect the pilot's concentration.'

Dominic sighed. 'Science is all gimmicks or proving things we already know. Sometimes I scare them on purpose.' His voice shrank to a whisper. 'At Bradford, crazy-fuck crosswinds hurl you about, the wings shake, you bounce up and down, everyone's terrified. So I wobble it a bit more so that when I touchdown,' he slapped his hand flat on the table. 'I get a round of applause.'

As If You Are There

I HAD A wife and the sound and smell of her was real. I believed I was immersed, but I wasn't.

I was outside of everything.

Then I visited Ryan's immersive art show. The colours are peanut M&Ms and you climb a swimming-pool ladder to get onto the sofa.

Ryan discovered that I like to be immersed. Sometimes it's not good for people to know what you like. It gives them power.

But this time it was all right.

I began to live in Ryan's art installation

and became part of the immersion. I speak to people and make them feel real.

I belong to Ryan, I'm his bitch. He makes me fight and steal things.

It is consumer uncanny.

Ryan says that if I get bored living in the installation I should jack my mind directly into the furiously pulsating heart of the internet, but I can't be bothered.

Talking to the Budgerigar

When I was fifteen I spoke to my younger sister's budgerigar for a long time about an unrequited love I harboured for a girl called Angela Watson who lived down past the farm.

I was out of my head on drugs most of the time back then, living on the edge really, and the budgerigar seemed to speak back to me, and it spoke a lot of sense: about life, and cages, and mirrors. It was a really existential experience, and the budgerigar asked me if I had thought about getting some big mirrors for my bedroom, because this strategy had really worked for him.

It meant there was no need to worry about searching for a real companion.

I took this on board and lived like that until I was thirty-three. Then I hired a professional cleaner to sort out my mirrors and fell in love with her.

The Happy Spore

As I left the bar a woman said, 'Cheer up. We are just spores in the machine.'

Why would being a spore cheer you up?

I wondered about that phrase all night as I roamed the city looking for Randal.

Randal says I take life too seriously and I'm unable to relax.

But we are here and then we are not and what's relaxing about that?

An Albanian interpreter I met at the Home Office said that if you allow your heart to lighten it will float up to the stars.

Randal doesn't take life seriously. But he

ghosts around the city at night prying on people and asking them questions like, what colour is the internet? Or, what does a river look like from underneath?

I found him on the canalside looking at a goose and told him about the woman.

'Which way did she go?' he said.

The Leaves Are Really Something Else

GAYNOR FOUND SOMETHING in Franny's jeans.

'Seven-fucking-teen!' she screamed at me. 'What about her music? That song about the leaves? This sickness is poisoning our estate from the guts up.'

She dropped the packet into my palm like it was a turd and I knew immediately it was one of mine.

I went to Franny's club and found the promoter I'd sold the gear to.

'Young Franny,' he said. 'Yes. That amazing song about the leaves. But the leaves, as you know, are really something else.'

I ignored this and told him I needed him to give Franny a job helping to run the night. He looked terrified but said he'd try, and I left him to ponder.

I would speak to Franny about the leaves because in my opinion songs should never be in code. Deliberately excluding people is unfair and those who aren't included will always fight back.

The Periphery is Everywhere

SHE SAID THE city reflected an urbanism steeped in the increasingly non-linear capitalist production of 'themed' urban atmospheres. Nature has re-emerged in the very substance of Manchester itself—it is urbanism *as* nature.

I said Manchester is always an ex-post reality. The periphery is everywhere.

She said emotions are triggered by constructed moods. Anxiety prevents simple phenomena from being described simply. Culture is the opaque substance that separates us from phenomena outside our control.

I said her resentment of me was so big I could get inside and walk around.

She said, yes, emotions can have spatial characteristics.

I said experience is an ambulation that concatenates multiple overlapping relations.

She said I was like a cat watching contemporary dance.

I said the felt reality of experience is interwoven at the fringes of perception with the conjunctively structured envelope of wave forms.

She couldn't think of anything to say to that.

The Underpass

SHE USED TO get the 11.

I thought about her rumbling up Dudley Road, over Perry Barr roundabout, down Aston Lane, through Sarehole Mill, into Billesley.

She'd see Swan Island.

I told her about the underpass. In the old days you could get from Snow Hill to the Bull Ring without crossing a road; it was all underpasses.

I think about the underpass a lot.

There wasn't anything in the underpass.

It was just a way through.

But I think about it.

I told her about the gentle slope, all the way up from St Martin's Church. If they'd kept the gentle slope they could have sent the buses round the back but they had to send them underneath and now there's an ugly hump so the double-deckers can get their shoulders through.

Maybe it's darker now. Maybe it rains more.

Everything's underneath, but the women seem to like it.

Two Columns

IT WAS AN abstract work called *Two Columns*, and Betty's father loved the way it confronted ideas about presence.

'Looks like it was painted by a poodle with a brush up its arse,' Betty's mother said, leaning it face-first against the wall.

Betty's father worked for the police, but in his spare time made oil paintings for a website where they were critiqued by middle-aged widows with warts and soft moustaches.

'You are so bold with cobalt, Terence,'

they said. 'The sea on your canvasses pulsates.'

Betty's mother believed her husband's interest in art disguised occult, long-culverted desires.

'Why not go the whole way and move in a young man?' she said. 'He'd watch costume dramas with me and joke about back passages.'

Betty's father swivelled the painting round to face the room.

'Look at how the artist uses Payne's Grey. It both gives and absorbs.'

'I wish *you* did,' Betty's mother said.

Eat Less Pastry

ROUGH PEOPLE LIVE in rough places and have rough hands.

Nice people live with trees and say hello how are you. They have clean, easy jobs in offices and don't have to haul sacks of shit and take it up the arse from poncy cunts in specs.

Rough people stick knives in each others eyes and are sick in wastepaper bins, all stringy green stuff.

Nice people have violin lessons.

Rough people's bosses twat them in the

face and, if they are still wearing that big ring, it's a cut as well a bruise.

Nice people play squeaky biscuit in hotel rooms.

That's where the empty packets come from.

A Dress Code For Modern Musicians

PEOPLE WHO WORK at the intersection of sculpture and sound must keep the midriff covered.

A squonk-step artist may remove his top hat within a restaurant.

Clothing that works well for yard-work may not be appropriate for micro-tonal tuba trios.

The clothing of folktronica artists should be pressed and never wrinkled.

Clothing that reveals your back is not appropriate for grindient.

Drone-wash artists may wear slacks that are similar to flannel pants OR dressy capris. Nice-looking 'dress' synthetic pants are also acceptable.

Musique-concrete artists should avoid sweatpants, bib overalls, spandex and form-fitting leggings.

Short, tight skirts that ride halfway up the thigh should be worn AT ALL TIMES for forest dub core.

Turtlenecks are acceptable for drummers in a free-improvisational situation.

Female micro-bionic sound artists may wear jeans if the rivets are hidden.

For ladies performing Turkish psychedelia only formal day dress with a hat or substantial fascinator is acceptable.